The printer whisperer

31 illustrated
surreal office stories

Marie Blanchet

Foreword

There is something fascinating about surrealism that could be horror, but is not only by virtue of everyone shrugging and acting like it's completely normal. This sort of worldbuilding is at the core of stories like the podcast *Welcome To Night Vale*, or the once-popular "office gothic" Tumblr meme. I've been thinking of writing something like that for a long time, and then 2020 happened. Seemingly overnight, the entire world seemed to be plunged into a new day-to-day that was exactly that: surreal, terrifying, and yet boringly mundane. This zine is a tribute to every weird day at the office.

Paperback ISBN 978-1-7751197-9-1
PDF ISBN 978-1-7386611-9-0

Legal deposit – Bibliothèque et Archives nationales du Québec, 2022

Legal deposit – Library and Archives Canada, 2022

A low sound blared through the office, rattling the coffee cup on my desk. Outside the windows was a beautiful seaside city, and a large boat just coming into port. I checked my watch.

"Huh," I remarked to my coworkers, who were all entranced by the unexpected sunny day. "Since when does the office land in Newport at noon? Weren't we assigned to London for another week?"

"Shit," muttered the intern, sprinting toward the engine room. A shift, and then we were in the fog again.

As one, my coworkers swivelled toward me. "Why the HECK did you say anything?"

At my old office, we used to gather the interns in the darkened break room and tell them about the ghost printer. It was trashed after the building was hit by lightning, but sometimes it still appeared in your available printer list, no matter what I.T. did to get rid of it.

The secretary swore that one time, during a power outage, it appeared on her desk. Then she blinked and it was gone. They said if you stayed too late in the evening, you could hear its tortured wheezing as it tried to complete its last, unfinished printing job...

KSSHPLUN

A low rumbling shook the walls of the office.

"Blooooood..."

The head designer groaned.

"Did you leave spell sheets in the photocopier overnight again?" he asked.

His colleague frowned at him. "That only happened once! You can't keep blaming me every time our machines turn sentient!"

"I can and I will," he replied. "I get bitten every time I change the ink."

He checked the printer, but it wasn't the source of the wailing this time.

"Guuuuys?" someone yelled from the kitchen, "The coffee machine's screen says, huh, out of blood..."

"Water," sighed the designer. "Just fill it with water."

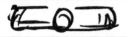

So I've been working at this small nonprofit for approaching five years. My email address is designer2@nameoffice.com.

There is no designer1. There's never been, and no one can tell me why the username is already taken on our server. But sometimes that account sends me emails. They are usually empty, with strange subjects lines and attachments I can't seem to be able to open. I answer them anyway, with polite office talk like "thank you for your input". It would be rude not to.

At least, unlike our boss, designer1 has never forgotten to email me on my birthday.

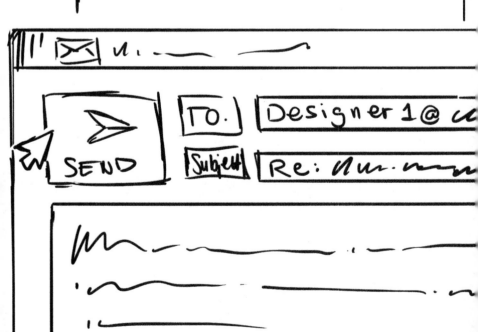

I started working at the office in spring.
Spring is our busiest time of the year.

That's what my coworkers told me, with
something approaching hysteria in their
eyes. I assumed it was lack of sleep.

It's been years now, but summer never came,
and neither did fall or winter. We held an
Easter party seven times, and one of them
we called Christmas as a joke. The business is
soaring. Spring is our busiest time of the year.

I've been working so many extra hours,
I forgot what my apartment and my cats
looked like. I wish June came.

There is someone snoring in the store, but the supervisor said to ignore it. I can hear it coming from behind the racks in the back store, I think.

According to the others, a client was locked in after closing time once, and they never found him again. They say he fell asleep into the "bed" section, but woke up in the night and wandered to "bath", and then "beyond". Maybe he fell back asleep there. It's been years. We can still hear him snore, but no one ever found him.

I don't remember us even having a back store.

For the last time, I am not Julia.

But I happened to be wearing a red shirt when the war started, and I was co-opted by the Target militia. They gave me her name tag. They said she was employee of the month ten times, and the badge would protect me.

The Walmart crew has captured territory again this morning. I just wanted a new pack of batteries. I miss my family, but Julia had a fantastic ham sandwich on rye bread in her lunch bag. It's not so bad being her.

I don't know what happened to Julia.

There are donuts on the table. Yesterday, there were bagels, and the day before that, muffins.

You've already had your fill. The very sight of another donut makes you gag. You want to stop eating, but you cannot.

You are the designated eater for the office. Terrible things will happen if there are leftovers. The other employees see that you are faltering, and they look at you with horror in their eyes.

"Maybe one more", edges an intern that you have never seen before. They take a chocolate donut, and you collapse in relief. Another eater has taken your place.

The office war started on Wednesday, when one of the fairies put up a "no fish in the employee's kitchen" sign. There might have been a prior provocation, but if so, no one would fess up to HR. In retaliation, the mermaids installed "no mammals" banners in the break room.

By the time Friday had rolled around, everyone seemed to have gotten involved. The Selkies were upset. The Kelpies refused to come to work.

The wood elves where the only ones not to take a side. When questioned, they replied that technically, they were neither fish nor mammals, but fungi.

NO FISH

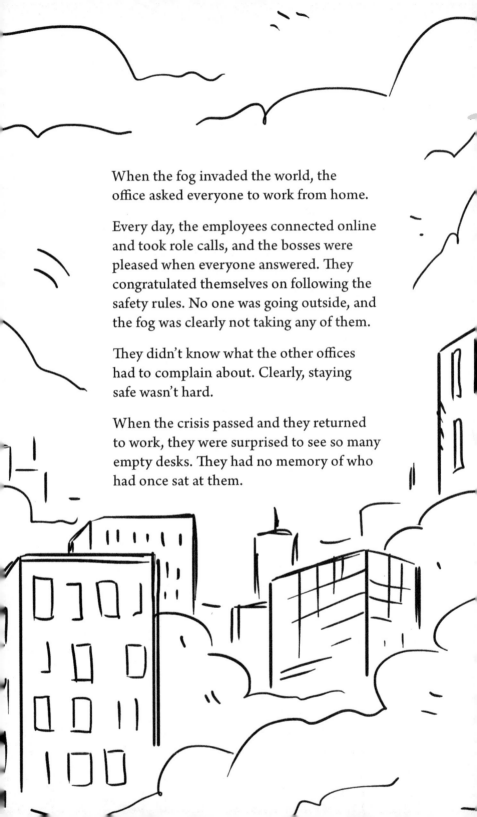

When the fog invaded the world, the
office asked everyone to work from home.

Every day, the employees connected online
and took role calls, and the bosses were
pleased when everyone answered. They
congratulated themselves on following the
safety rules. No one was going outside, and
the fog was clearly not taking any of them.

They didn't know what the other offices
had to complain about. Clearly, staying
safe wasn't hard.

When the crisis passed and they returned
to work, they were surprised to see so many
empty desks. They had no memory of who
had once sat at them.

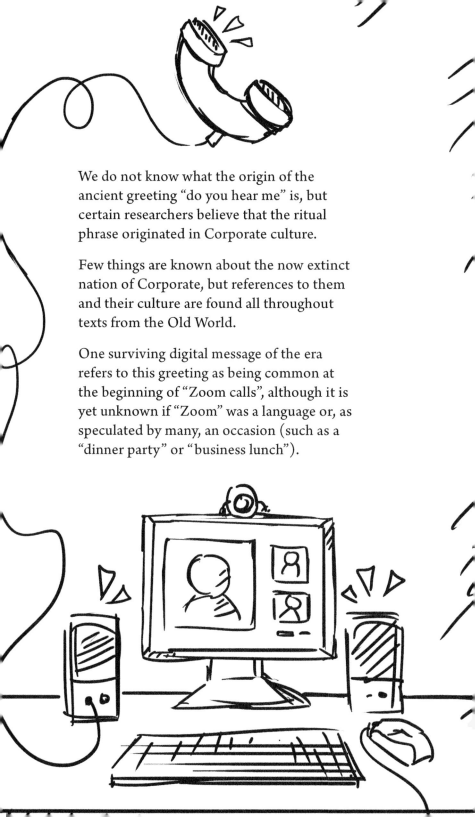

We do not know what the origin of the ancient greeting "do you hear me" is, but certain researchers believe that the ritual phrase originated in Corporate culture.

Few things are known about the now extinct nation of Corporate, but references to them and their culture are found all throughout texts from the Old World.

One surviving digital message of the era refers to this greeting as being common at the beginning of "Zoom calls", although it is yet unknown if "Zoom" was a language or, as speculated by many, an occasion (such as a "dinner party" or "business lunch").

"So, weird year, huh?" began the CEO of Agricorps Incorporated, to a smattering of laughs and applauses from his gathered employees. "I don't know about you guys, but for a moment there I really thought we were done for! Alright, let's see the highlights of this last semester…"

He gestured, and the first slide of his powerpoint presentation appeared on the giant screen behind him.

"We begin strong in June with the alien invasion… Fortunately we quickly learn that our new overlords loooove gardening on board of their generation ships, so we were able to develop a promising new market…"

"It's nice to be working outside, for once," said Henchmen Number One, squinting up at the sun and rearranging their laptop screen. "Shame the office was destroyed, though."

"There never was an office," said Number Two. "Remember? It was an hallucination to demoralize those heroes by making them think they had a crappy normal life."

"Oh," said Henchmen Number Three, glancing down at her laptop and the extensive spreadcheet she'd been putting together. "Are we still getting paid, then?"

"I am," said Number One, pulling up their banking website.

"That's all that matters, then," she shrugged, returning to her spreadcheet.

So, funny story, but I honestly thought I was working at a mafia front at first. I've only met the owner one time when she hired me, and we almost never have any customers.

The people who do come in tend to ask for stuff with weird-ass names like "dragon's breath" and "unicorn powder". Now, I'm not a big fan of selling drugs, but I've never had a customer come back twice, so I figured it was no big deal.

But then – get this – one day, this guy came over and said he was with the witches' union.

"For the last time," said the girl at the desk across from me, "you need to kill the Queen or your problem will keep coming back!"

She listened to whoever was at the other end of her phone for a moment, then typed something into her computer.

I wished I hadn't left my noise cancelling headphones at home. Now that my department was sitting near the YA phone support, I could never get any work done without being distracted.

"What do you mean, you're in love?" she said exasperatedly.

I sighed and tried to focus back on my own work.

We're pretty lucky that the ghost that haunts the third floor of the building is territorial. I mean, sure, she eats people from time to time, but it's mostly interns. And the death rattle gets easy to ignore after a while.

I'm saying this because there's been a wave of spam emails lately. You know, those messages that you need to forward or else a little death gremlin comes to murder you. Those emails.

A ton of our competitors have gone under already, by cause of "everyone got killed". But not us! Our very own ghost ate the gremlin, apparently.

"So, welcome to Paradox and Sons, esq." said our new boss. "I hope you like your time here. Today, you'll be helping the senior attorneys research for their court cases. Let's see…"

He looked down at his files and shuffled some things around.

"So we have a woman who says that she can't be charged with murdering her husband, because he came back to life. We also have a man who arrived here via illegal time travel, but argues that it was legal when he left. Any takers?"

I exchanged an excited glance with my best friend. Best internship ever!

The problem with small towns is that you're bound to run into people you know at the store. You kind of hate that.

It takes you a long time, though, to realize that you never meet your coworkers when grocery shopping. It's a big office, you should logically run into one of them eventually, yeah? It takes you even longer to notice that your fridge is always full, and your clothes always clean. There's not really any need to go outside anymore...

Huh, guess they really weren't joking when they said that the corporate family would take care of you.

GROCERY LIST

The first thing you need to know about
Mark from accounting is that he always
sends unnecessarily complicated Excel
spreadsheets.

The second thing you need to know is that
the information you're looking for will
always be in the first rows and columns,
and you shouldn't ever scroll to look at
the last few ones.

There's nothing dangerous about them, but
they can get weird. The date of your death,
for example. The name of your childhood
imaginary friend. He doesn't mean any harm
by it, it's just that his psychic powers act up
sometimes. It could happen to anyone.

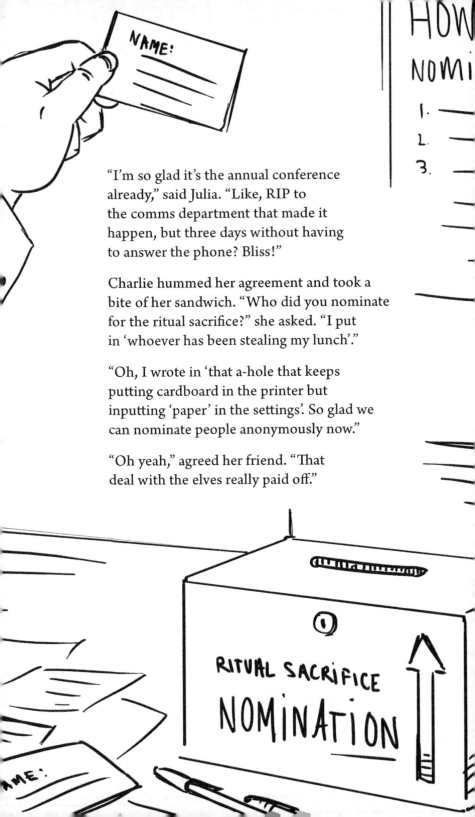

NAME:

"I'm so glad it's the annual conference already," said Julia. "Like, RIP to the comms department that made it happen, but three days without having to answer the phone? Bliss!"

Charlie hummed her agreement and took a bite of her sandwich. "Who did you nominate for the ritual sacrifice?" she asked. "I put in 'whoever has been stealing my lunch'."

"Oh, I wrote in 'that a-hole that keeps putting cardboard in the printer but inputting 'paper' in the settings'. So glad we can nominate people anonymously now."

"Oh yeah," agreed her friend. "That deal with the elves really paid off."

RITUAL SACRIFICE
NOMINATION

NAME:

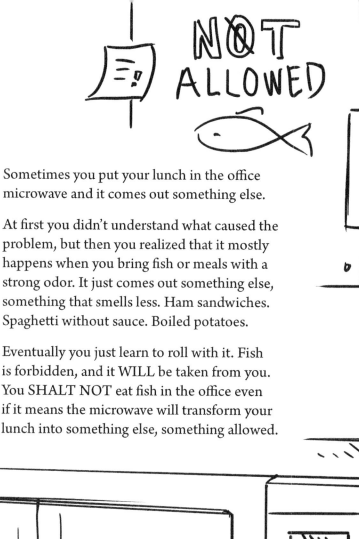

NOT ALLOWED

Sometimes you put your lunch in the office microwave and it comes out something else.

At first you didn't understand what caused the problem, but then you realized that it mostly happens when you bring fish or meals with a strong odor. It just comes out something else, something that smells less. Ham sandwiches. Spaghetti without sauce. Boiled potatoes.

Eventually you just learn to roll with it. Fish is forbidden, and it WILL be taken from you. You SHALT NOT eat fish in the office even if it means the microwave will transform your lunch into something else, something allowed.

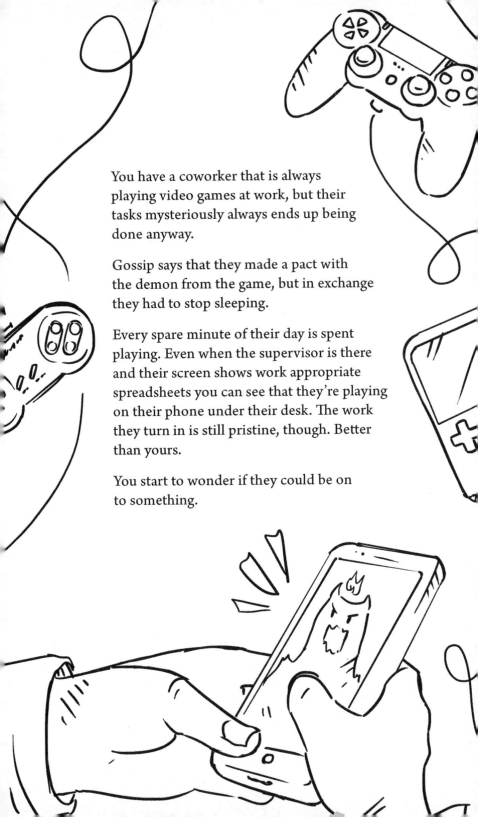

You have a coworker that is always playing video games at work, but their tasks mysteriously always ends up being done anyway.

Gossip says that they made a pact with the demon from the game, but in exchange they had to stop sleeping.

Every spare minute of their day is spent playing. Even when the supervisor is there and their screen shows work appropriate spreadsheets you can see that they're playing on their phone under their desk. The work they turn in is still pristine, though. Better than yours.

You start to wonder if they could be on to something.

The water in the office building tastes strange, but you have never managed to put your finger on exactly what is off about it. It's different from home, you can tell that clearly.

You don't feel well when you drink it, and you pee more than usual. Your coworkers wont touch it. When you ask about the water, they don't answer your questions, but they are insistent, and their eyes are wild.

"Have coffee instead. You will concentrate better."

You switch to coffee. After several cups you've forgotten all about the water. It doesn't seem much of a problem anymore.

There's a child in the office. Is it bring your child to work day? Is there a school holiday that you didn't know about, and their parent couldn't find a babysitter? You don't know. You didn't even know that your coworkers had children.

But there's a child, and no one is acknowledging them. They are playing on a handheld console and being very quiet, so you try to ignore them too. When you turn back around, they're gone. You ask, and no one knows what you are talking about.

There was never a child here. Management would never allow it.

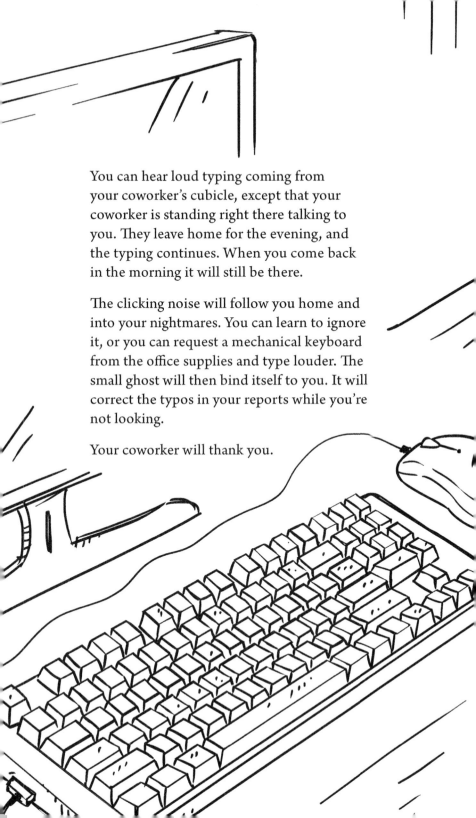

You can hear loud typing coming from your coworker's cubicle, except that your coworker is standing right there talking to you. They leave home for the evening, and the typing continues. When you come back in the morning it will still be there.

The clicking noise will follow you home and into your nightmares. You can learn to ignore it, or you can request a mechanical keyboard from the office supplies and type louder. The small ghost will then bind itself to you. It will correct the typos in your reports while you're not looking.

Your coworker will thank you.

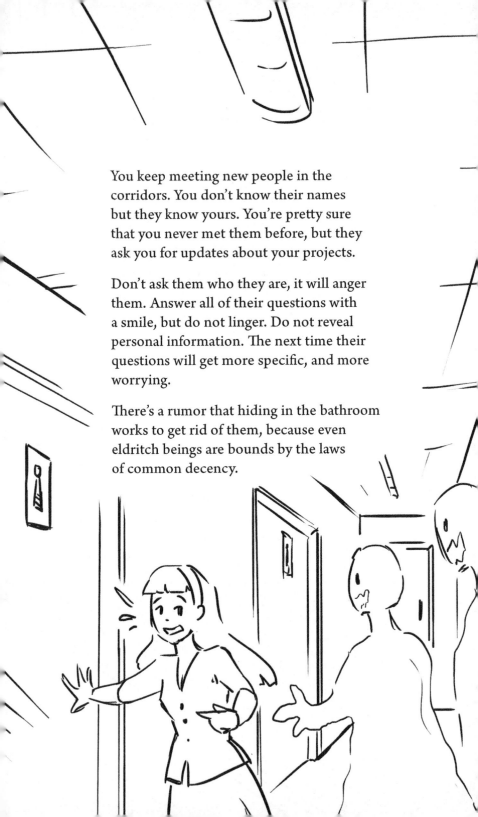

You keep meeting new people in the corridors. You don't know their names but they know yours. You're pretty sure that you never met them before, but they ask you for updates about your projects.

Don't ask them who they are, it will anger them. Answer all of their questions with a smile, but do not linger. Do not reveal personal information. The next time their questions will get more specific, and more worrying.

There's a rumor that hiding in the bathroom works to get rid of them, because even eldritch beings are bounds by the laws of common decency.

The trust and team building exercises that management is making you do are getting weirder and weirder. They send you to boot camp. They make you learn the sword. Every year at the Christmas party, they wait until everyone is drunk to pick a name out of a hat, and that one is the Chosen One and the rest of you are his army. It's all good fun. Every year when summer rolls around the supervisors gather in the breakroom.

"It hasn't happened yet," they say. "We're safe for a while longer".

They send everyone to yet another training camp.

You come back to the parking lot and your car isn't where you left it. It's much further away from the doors. You walk a lot longer than it feels like you should to reach it, and as you leave you get a call from a coworker that an emergency has happened and you need to go back up to your office.

Do not.

The coworker in question has already gone home. The building does not want you to leave, but you have to be strong. It's dangerous to still be there after sundown.

Also your extra hours aren't paid.

RULES

One morning, management installs a new rule. You MUST remove your boots and shoes in the locker room and only go up into the upper floors with soft slippers.

The slippers are provided, at least, but they come out of your paycheck. You mustn't make any noise in the office, or raise your voice above a whisper. Phone calls are now prohibited except in certain areas, and you're told to use the text chat app to talk with your coworkers as much as possible.

It is imperative that you do not disturb the open space. DO NOT wake the beast.

Ever since the fairy market opened next door, I've had the hardest time preventing my employees from doing dumb shit. Just this morning, I emailed one of our designers a request which I ended with a friendly "just use your imagination! ;)"

She replied: "I don't have any. Sold it to a witch to cure my insomnia."

What does that even mean?!

Oh, for – My assistant just texted me that she'd be late because she "exchanged her sense of time for infinite paninis." That's it! I'm going down to the market myself. I need to put a stop to this nonsense.

FAIRY ⇨
MARKET

Like the rest of their culture, the Martian concept of fast food isn't about speed so much as being about efficiency.

They want to be able to tell you "I'm going to do [thing]" and you'll dish out the exact kind of nutrition needed for the situation. No choosing or thinking needed, thank you, next.

After years of low self-esteem in your youth, you're great a counting calories. You look at people and you know exactly how much they're gonna need. That's not what you thought high school would prepare you for, but hey. You work with what you have.

Thanks for reading!

For more books and zines, subscribe
to my monthly newsletter at
rebrand.ly/BLAM_EN

Find me on social media!

 @blam.marie

 @blammarie.bsky.social

 blog.blanchetmarie.com

Further reading...

THE BLOOD PRINCE

It started with a betrayal.
It will end in flames.

SKIN DEEP

One Selkie.
Two strangers.
Three murders.

KALIPSO

When fantasy meets
science-fiction...

SNAPSHOTS FROM THE SEA

31 illustrated short stories
on the theme of mermaids

blanchetmarie.com

Printed in Great Britain
by Amazon

43763508R00030